TEACH THE CLARINET

4.95

TEACH THE CLARINET

Nigel Keates

Stainer and Bell

First published in Great Britain by
Stainer & Bell Ltd, 82 High Road, London N2 9PW

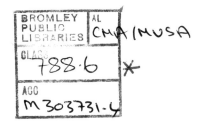

Keates, Nigel
   Teach the clarinet.
   1. Clarinet—Instruction and study—
Handbooks, manuals etc.
   I. Title
   788'.62'0712   MT380

ISBN 0-85249-609-5

Printed in Great Britain by Galliard (Printers) Ltd, Great Yarmouth

Contents

Introduction

There are many clarinet tutors for student beginners: this book aims to help the new **teacher** as well. The methodical steps can be used whatever 'method' the teacher has inherited, providing 150 exercises progressing through the steps to Grade 3 examination level. Each step has daily warm-ups and in the whole book 98 tunes—some well-known, some specially composed by the author—form a basic repertory for students, taught individually or in groups.

Great emphasis is placed throughout on good tone and intonation, both depending on careful listening and inner hearing. In many countries, it is common practice for every music student to study *solfège*, an elaborate and systematic study of basic musicianship based on the relation of fixed intervals originally intended for singers to sing in tune. In other countries, the moveable 'doh' system devised by John Curwen in 19th-century England has been acknowledged as an early aid to reading music, particularly for singers and string players in Hungary as adapted by Kodaly. Recently The New Curwen Method (published by Stainer and Bell for the Curwen Institute) has led to a revival in English-speaking countries.

Teachers are strongly recommended to encourage young clarinettists to think in the basic solfa arpeggio of 'doh-me-soh' from the beginning so that they can hear notes in the ear before their fingers and the instrument actually produce the sound. An intelligent student may go quite a long way purely on the sight of a musical symbol and a digital response on the instrument but unless the sound can be correctly imagined *before* it is heard, there will be problems ahead in what is termed 'musicianship'. Musicianship is inseparable from the act of playing and to this end, teachers are here reminded of the importance of reading, of memorising, of writing what is heard and on playing *by ear*.

The student has time to concentrate on specific problems without becoming bored; the inexperienced teacher is saved hours of preparation in trying to find suitable practice material; and the experienced teacher may still find the book a useful compendium for a student to work through, however successful a method the teacher has evolved from his or her years in the profession.

2

The routine for each step is usually:

    (a) advice to the teacher
    (b) warm-up exercise for the student to use daily
    (c) preliminary exercises on the title of the step
    (d) tunes incorporating the teaching points in the exercises of (c)
    (e) supplementary exercises taking the step further
    (f) more tunes illustrating the points in the whole step

Enjoy your lessons, teaching or being taught.

N. K.
London, 1984

The range of notes is shown in the text as follows:

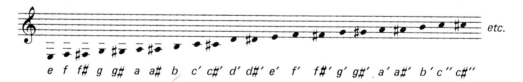

Keys are shown in capitals: C, G, B♭, etc.

The line drawings are by Jenny Cecil, to whom the author is most indebted.
The book is dedicated to his greatly valued teacher, the late Yona Ettlinger.

Step 1: Left Hand Notes

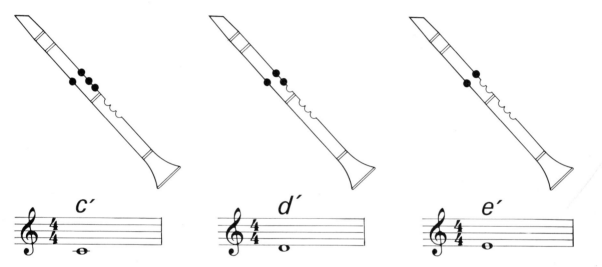

TEACHING NOTES

Make sure that your students know the relative values of ♩, ♩ and o notes and rests as shown in the first rhythm exercise. It may help at first to sing '1, 2, 3, 4' and clap the notes, then count *silently* while the exercise is played.

The first four Preliminary Exercises should be used as a daily warm-up. Using solfa in the mind, students should first sing out loud 'doh' and 'me' (a major third) checking the pitch of 'doh' by playing c' then *think* 'doh' or 'me' as indicated. In all the exercises 'doh' is shown at the beginning by □ and 'me' as ● above it.

Apart from this emphasis on listening for tonic intonation from the beginning, the teaching points to be made in this step are:

    (a) starting and sustaining the tone (Preliminary Exercises)
    (b) articulating the different note values using the tongue (the Rhythmic Exercises)
    (c) synchronising the tongue and fingers (the Supplementary Exercises)
    (d) beginning to memorise (the Tunes)

RHYTHM EXERCISE

There are four values in each bar. The value 𝅗𝅥 lasts for two 𝅘𝅥. The value o lasts for four 𝅘𝅥. Count and play, thinking the note 'me' in solfa. Write out similar exercises, making up 8 bars of four 𝅘𝅥-value exercises, learning the symbols for the rests of similar lengths, (𝅘𝅥 = 𝄽, 𝅗𝅥 = ▬, o = ▬).

Doh is C

PRELIMINARY EXERCISES

Doh is C

1 Think 'doh'

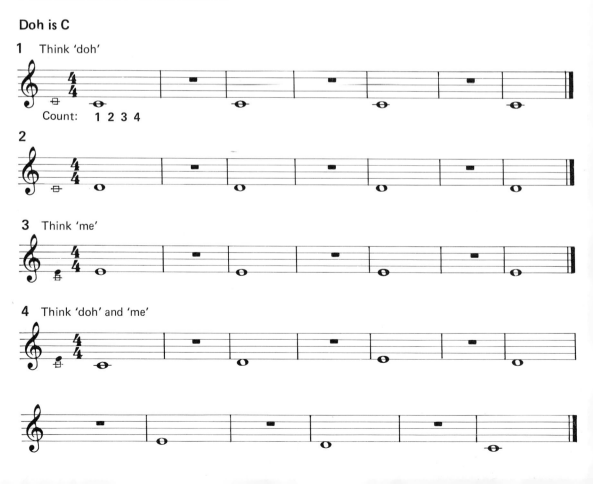

2

3 Think 'me'

4 Think 'doh' and 'me'

RHYTHM TEASERS

First sing these to 'la': this will help to *think* rhythmically with the tongue.

Doh is C

SUPPLEMENTARY EXERCISES

8

TUNES

First sing the tunes to 'la', thinking also of the pitches 'me' and 'doh' and fingering the notes on the clarinet at the same time. Then play them until you know the tunes by heart.

Pots and Pans

Doh is C

N.K.

Merrily we roll along

Doh is C

Trad.

Tammy's Tune

Doh is C

N.K.

When you can play the tunes by heart, write them out on manuscript paper from memory, letting the clarinet remind you if your memory fails.

Step 2:   Right Hand Notes

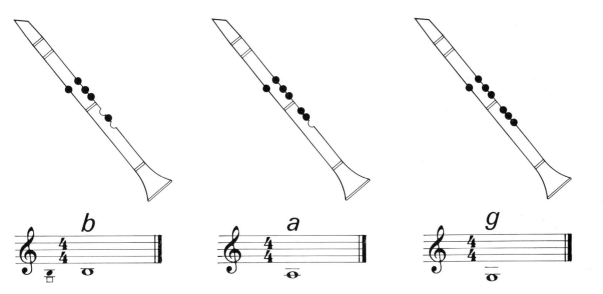

TEACHING NOTES

The first four Preliminary Exercises should again be used as a daily warm-up. In solfa terms 'doh' is *g* in the Preliminary Exercises. As before, students should play *g* and sing it as the new 'doh', thinking and then singing 'me' above it before playing *b*.

Technical teaching points to be made are the same as in Step 1. The notes *b, a* and *g* have been preferred at this stage to the more usual thumb *f* and open *g* as the student will not need to bite to keep the clarinet steady.

PRELIMINARY EXERCISES

Doh is G

1 Think 'me'

2

3 Think 'doh'

4 Think 'me' and 'doh'

5

6

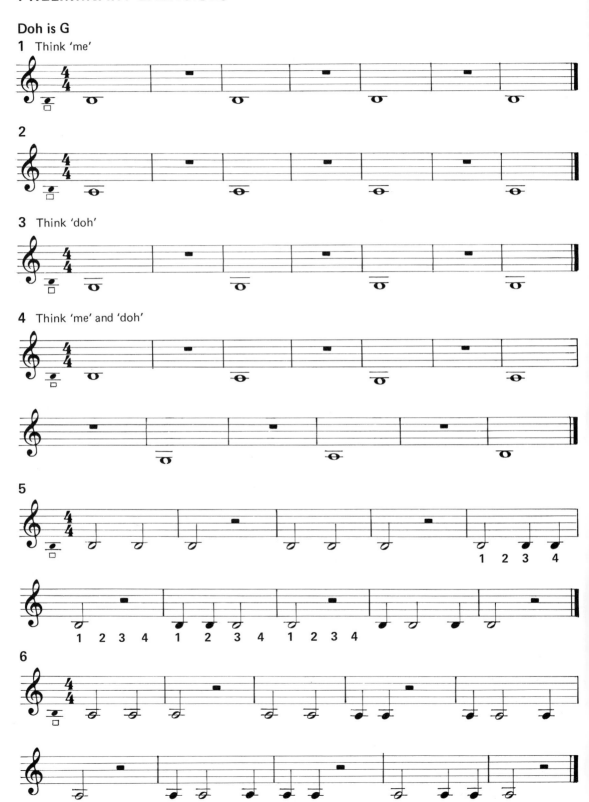

7

8

RHYTHM TEASERS

Doh is G

1

2

12

3

4

SUPPLEMENTARY EXERCISES

Doh is C

1

2

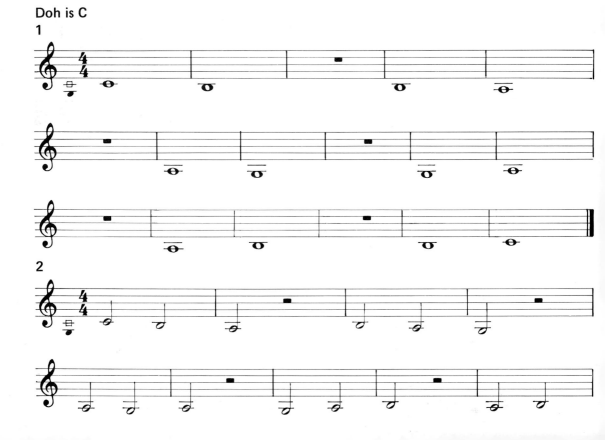

3

4

TUNES

Sing before playing as before.

Merrily we roll along

Doh is G   Trad.

Simple Syncopation

Doh is G

N.K.

On and On

Doh is C

Practise singing 'soh' *below* 'doh' (a fourth). Think 'doh' and low 'soh' as you play.

N.K.

When you can play the tunes by heart, write them out from memory. Particularly in the long 'On and On' notice the shape of the tune by looking at the first note of all the odd-numbered bars (1, 3, 5 and so on).

Step 3:   Left and Right Hands Combined

TEACHING NOTES

The Supplementary Exercises and Tunes in Step 2 re-introduced left hand *c'* with the three right hand notes. In this step, all three left hand notes of Step 1 are combined with those of Step 2.

Now that the student understands that 'doh' can move from one note to another the key-signature is introduced for 'doh is G' in *A Sad Song.* It is unnecessary to explain all the complications of key-signatures at this stage. As long as students know that one sharp in the key-signature means 'doh is G' they will be prepared to learn *why* later. (In any case, some students may already have learnt another instrument on which they have met key-signatures before.) Students should sing 'me-doh-soh₁' in C and 'doh-me-soh' in G to hear the different keys clearly.

All the exercises should be practised aiming for evenness of tone from note to note. All notes are intended to be tongued. Do not go on to Step 4 until the student has really good facility in the exercises up to now.

16

DAILY WARM-UPS

A dot after the value ♩ means that it lasts half as long again *ie* ♩. = 3 × ♪.

Doh is C
1

1 2 3 4 1 2 3 4

Doh is C
2

PRELIMINARY EXERCISES

Doh is C

TUNES

Hymn without words

Doh is C

N.K.

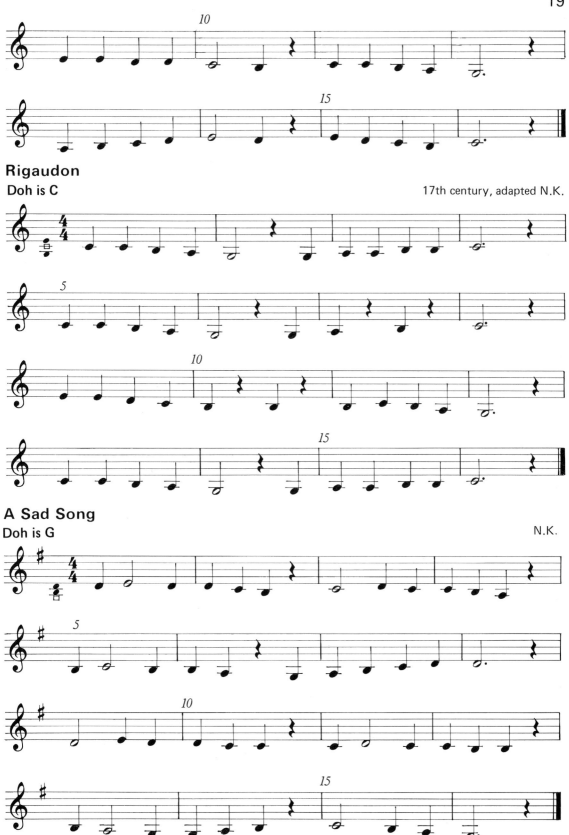

Rigaudon
Doh is C

17th century, adapted N.K.

A Sad Song
Doh is G

N.K.

Step 4:   Intervals

TEACHING NOTES

All the intervals played so far have been 'seconds'—tones or semitones next to each other—with only one finger to move between one and the other. This step gives material requiring neat co-ordination of two, three and four fingers with the tongue, in changing notes a third, fourth and fifth apart.

DAILY WARM-UP

Doh is C

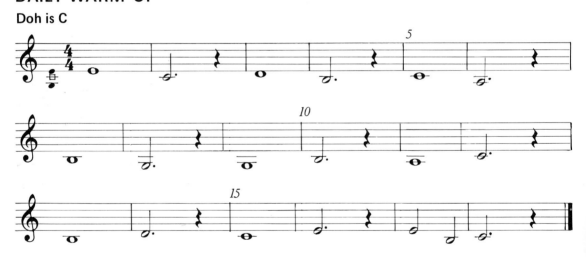

PRELIMINARY EXERCISES

These are both in thirds in C major.

Doh is C

1

TUNES

These all involve thirds in G major.

Hey Lolly

Doh is G

Trad. Caribbean

Aunt Rhody

Doh is G

Trad. adapted N.K.

Lightly Row

Doh is G

Trad. adapted N.K.

Michael, Row the Boat Ashore

Doh is G

Trad. adapted N.K.

Jolly Polly

Doh is G

N.K.

SUPPLEMENTARY EXERCISES

This is all in fourths. Sing it first to 'la', fingering the notes, thinking of 'me-doh-soh₁', as they are shown at the beginning.

1

Doh is C

This mixes thirds, fourths and fifths. Sing it first to 'la', fingering the notes, thinking of 'me-doh-soh₁'.

2

Doh is C

TUNES

These mix all the intervals practised so far in the keys of C and G. Sing, play, memorise; and write them out afterwards from memory.

Au Clair de la Lune

Doh is C

Trad.

Old Macdonald had a Farm

Doh is C

Trad. adapted N.K.

Good King Wenceslas

Doh is C

Piae Cantiones (1582) adapted N.K.

In the last two tunes, the notes in the last bar but one are not the original tune. Can you play the correct version? Then write it down.

This Old Man

Doh is G Trad. adapted N.K.

In bars 5 and 6, the traditional words are 'Nick, nack, paddy-wack, give a dog a bone'. Try to supply the missing notes as you play.

Hop, Skip and Jump

Doh is G N.K.

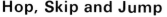

Twinkle, Twinkle, Little Star

Doh is G Trad. adapted N.K.

D. C. al Fine = 'from the start to the finishing line' in Italian. Go back to the beginning and play it again until *Fine*.

Police Constable Plod

Doh is C

N.K.

Step 5: Thumb Note F; B Flat and Bottom F

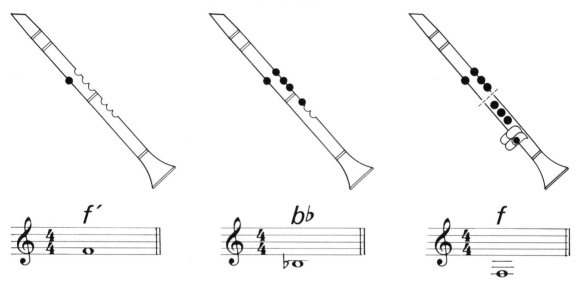

TEACHING NOTES

In this Step, 'doh' moves again, first to F and then to B flat. Note the new key-signatures. When the student reaches the second exercise in F, the visible reason for the key-signature symbol becomes clear: the *b* in the exercise is always flat—the middle of the three new notes now being used for the first time. In the Finger Stretcher, 'doh' is B flat: the key-signature shows that, *if there were* any notes *e'*, they would be $e^{b'}$ just as the *b*'s are $b^{b'}$. Although this exercise has no notes *e'*, students will begin to remember: **always look at the key-signature before you read**.

Technically, the student should now be ready to play thumb *f'* without biting the mouthpiece and, with the introduction of b^b and bottom *f*, will be able to play the natural scale of the clarinet: F major. From this step onwards, scales and arpeggios ('doh-me-soh-doh$^{l'}$) are introduced for each new key and should form part of daily practice.

DAILY WARM-UP

This is a revision exercise on the six notes already in the student's knowledge, before introducing the new notes of this step.

Doh is C

PRELIMINARY EXERCISES

Doh is F

1

Thinking 'doh-soh', what note would you play instead of the last 𝄽 to finish off the exercise?

2

THE FINGER TWISTER

Doh is F

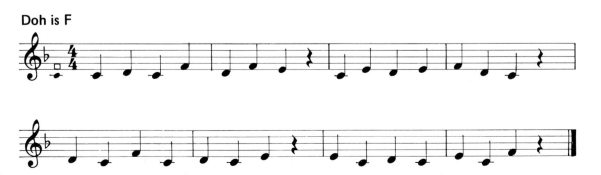

SUPPLEMENTARY EXERCISES

Doh is F

1

Doh is F

2   The Scale of F major

Arpeggio of F major

Doh is F

3

Arpeggio of F major

Play the next exercise very slowly at first, listening carefully and checking that every 'doh', 'me' and 'soh' is in tune.

4   The Scale of F major in 'broken thirds'

THE FINGER STRETCHER

Doh is B flat

TUNES

Balmy Evening

Doh is F

N.K.

Abide with Me

Doh is F

W.H. Monk, 1823 - 89

Note that in bar 7, the composer adds ♮ before *b*. This cancels the ♭ in the key-signature and this note *b* alone in the piece is *b natural* (for fingering, see Step 2).

Jingle Bells

After bar 6 play the bars marked ⌐1 and repeat from the beginning at the sign :‖.
Second time round, play the 'second time' bars, marked ⌐2 .

Doh is F   Trad.

Circus March

Doh is F   N.K.

Step 6:   Revision

TEACHING NOTES

In consolidating the previous Steps, the new time signature of three ♩-value beats in a bar is introduced. The construction of a time signature (top numeral = number of beats; lower numeral = value of beats in relation to 𝅝), is best explained here. When students write the tunes from memory, they can re-write some of them in $\frac{3}{2}$ time to appreciate the different 'look' of $\frac{3}{2}$. Then the point must be made that one is not necessarily slower than the other: speed depends on the length of the longest—or shortest—note. Encourage students to play in different tempos from this step onwards.

The routine of singing to 'la', of thinking, fingering, playing and memorising should continue in all practice.

DAILY WARM-UP

Doh is F

PRELIMINARY EXERCISES

Doh is F

5

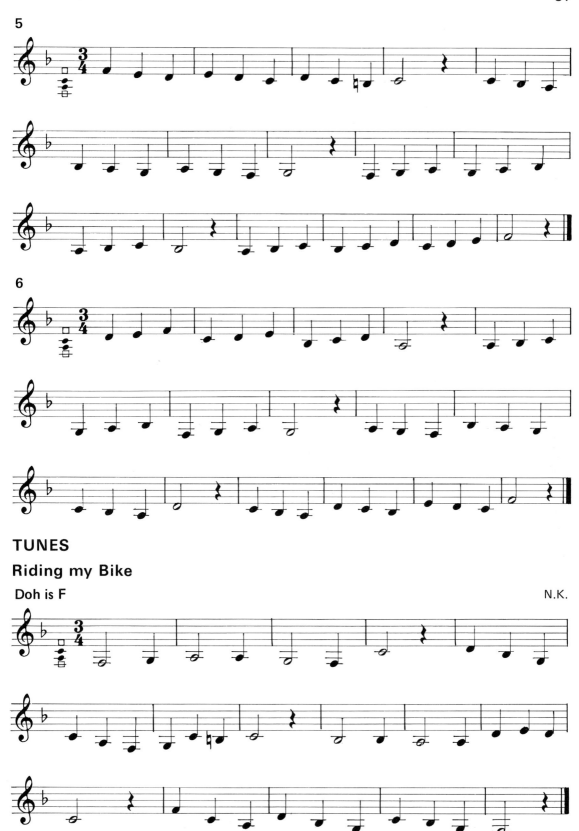

6

TUNES

Riding my Bike

Doh is F

N.K.

Boys and Girls come out to play

Doh is G

Trad.

√ means 'take a quick breath'.

Vilikins and his Dinah

Doh is F

Trad.

A Charabanc Ride

Doh is G

N.K.

Encourage students to find out what a 'charabanc' was—and why it was called a 'char-a-banc'.

The Man on the Flying Trapeze

Doh is C

Alfred Lee

Oops!

(> is used to mark a heavy fall on to the note, or 'accent'.)

Up in a Balloon

Doh is C   N.K.

Samantha's Song

Doh is F   N.K.

Step 7: Open G, F Sharp and Bottom F Sharp

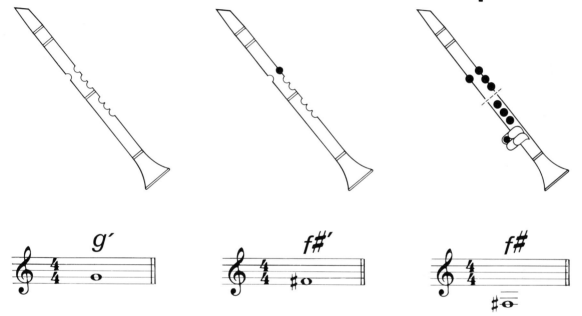

TEACHING NOTES

The warm-up acts as revision of notes already used. Note that ♮ only affects the bar in which it occurs and that in bar 6, *b* is flat. From the first of the Preliminary Exercises, the aim is to practise playing the open *g'* *in tune* when the left hand thumb is removed. See that the student's clarinet or embouchure does not move. Clear tone and true intonation may be helped by balancing the mouthpiece against the upper teeth. Solfa thinking of *g'* either as 'soh' in C major or 'doh' in G major gives the ear a note to check intonation against, immediately the clarinet produces the sound.

Remind the student that ♮ cancels ♯ only in the bar where it occurs. In Preliminary Exercise 3 all *f*'s *without* ♮ are *f♯'* because the key-signature indicates it; in the previous exercise all *f*'s are sharp.

DAILY WARM-UP

Doh is F

PRELIMINARY EXERCISES

1

Doh is C

2
Doh is G

3
Doh is G

4 The Scale of G major

Arpeggio of G major

5
Doh is G

6
Doh is G

7   The Scale of G major, broken thirds

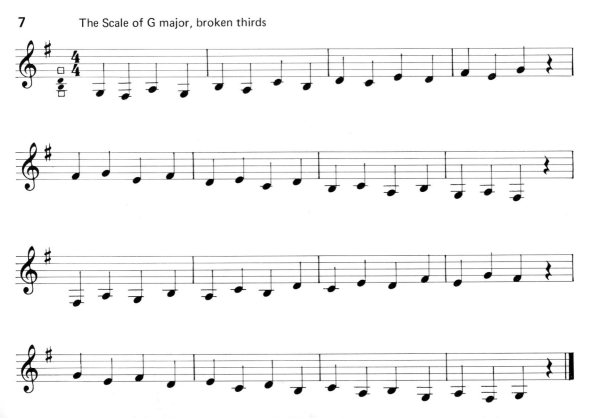

TUNES

The Peckham Polka

Doh is G

N.K.

Idle Man Blues

Doh is G

N.K.

The Coventry Carol

All *f*s which are to be played *f♯* have this indicated as the key-signature does not show otherwise. Key-signatures never mix sharps and flats. When this produces a mixture of key in sound, as here, the key is usually a **minor key**. In this tune, the key-signature therefore shows that 'doh' is B♭ but the sound rests more on a 'home note' of G.

Doh is B flat (Key is G minor)
Medieval Carol

When you have learned this carol by heart, try altering the last note to B flat and let your ear hear this as 'doh'. Then play it again, making the last note G. This will help to hear the 'minor' effect. Finally, play *Idle Man Blues* again and hear that 'doh' is clearly *g* and *g'*: the *b♭* in this tune is what jazz musicians call a 'blue' note.

Step 8: The Values and ♪♪♪♪

TEACHING NOTES

The new warm-up is intended to help the student to aim at exactly the same tone quality and intonation on the third *c'* of each group as the first. To do this, the embouchure must remain perfectly still while the ears must be hyper-active.

The exercises are technically simple so that students can concentrate entirely in sub-dividing the beats. As in Step 1, singing and clapping may well give some students more confidence. "Look for the beams", *ie* the lines joining stems, is a good maxim and writing out the tunes from memory will also make this aspect of sightreading stick in the mind. Do not let the student play these exercises too quickly: speed is less important than clarity of articulation and maintenance of pitch, as in the warm-up.

DAILY WARM-UP

Doh is C

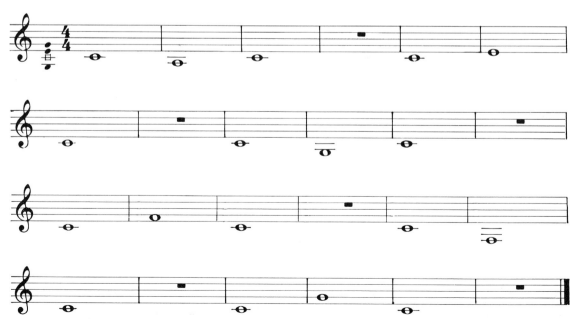

PRELIMINARY EXERCISES

1

Doh is F

Count: 1 2 3 4 & 1 2 3 4

1 2 & 3 4 1 2 3 4 1 2 3 4

2 The Scale of F major

1 2 3 4

3 The Scale of G major

1 2 3 4

1 & 2 3 4

4 The Scale of G major

1 2 3 4 1 2 3 4

1 2 3 4

5 The Scale of F major

7

Doh is F

TUNES

Nursery Rhyme

Doh is G   Trad.

Papa a du Tabac

Doh is C   Trad. adapted N.K.

FINE

D.C. al FINE

A Pearl for Shirl

Listen particularly in bar 4 and ask yourself if you hear a change of 'doh'. if you do, the tune has changed to the key of G here—called 'modulation'—but it does not change the key of the whole tune which ends firmly on 'doh is C' *ie* the key of C major.

Doh is C   N.K.

Clarinet Take-away

In this tune 'doh' may again be *c'*, but it is less clearly the 'home note'. Many folktunes—in the West and in the East—use five-note scales (called 'pentatonic') in which any one of the five notes may be the home note. So this piece is pentatonic.

N.K.

When you have memorised this tune, write out the names of the five notes used—F, G, A, C, D—and put them on the stave. In this way, you will see that, in the tune, G is used in two octaves, but the others only in one.

Polly Wolly Doodle

Doh is C

Trad.

Step 9:   Revision Tunes

TEACHING NOTES

These well-known tunes include some rounds if you are able to group your students. They are intended to provide both recapitulation and recreation. Some students will be keen to go on to Step 10: do not hold them back. Others may need the revision—or simply want to increase the number of tunes they 'know'.

The only additional notation symbol to be explained is the tie in *Land of my Fathers*.

Flow gently, sweet Afton

Doh is C

Trad. adapted N.K.

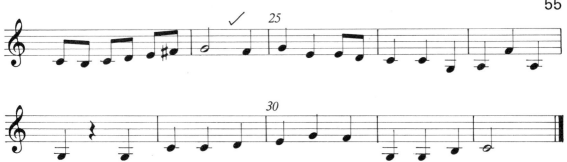

O, no, John!

Doh is C

The Vicar of Bray

Doh is F

17th-century Ballad Tune

Hot Cross Buns

Doh is C

Trad. adapted N.K.

London's Burning (Round)

Doh is C

16th-century English

Little Tommy Tinker (Round)

Doh is G

N.K.

Ye Sportive Birds (Round)

Doh is C

18th-century Glee

Lavender's Nearly Blue

Doh is G

Trad. adapted N.K.

Land of my Fathers

Doh is G

James James (Ieuan ap Ieuan), 1833 - 1902

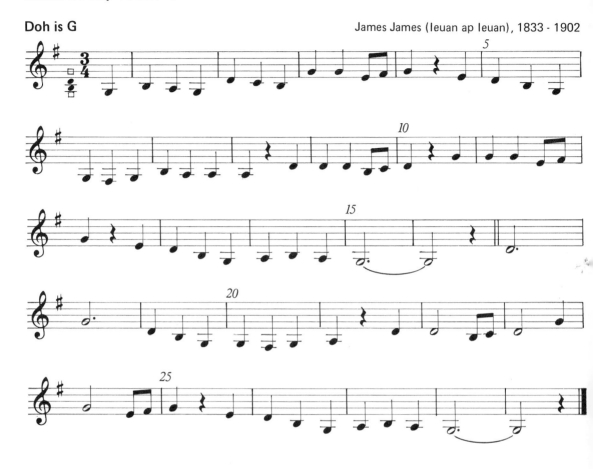

Shortnin' Bread

Doh is F

Trad. adapted N.K.

John Peel

Doh is G

19th-century ballad

Step 10: Bottom E

e

TEACHING NOTES

The Preliminary Exercises approach bottom e (left hand little finger) through bottom f (right hand little finger) and are designed to develop co-ordination of the little fingers. The Supplementary Exercises approach bottom e through bottom $f^{\sharp}$ which needs separate practice. You may wish to point out that in the second Supplementary Exercise the left hand little finger may remain depressed throughout. All these exercises should be practised in strict tempo, even if this means a very slow ♩ beat to accommodate the values ♫♫ .

DAILY WARM-UP

Doh is C

PRELIMINARY EXERCISES

1
Doh is F

2
Doh is C

3
Doh is C

4
Doh is F

5
Doh is F

6
Doh is F

7
Doh is F

TUNES

Come, Landlord, fill the flowing Bowl

Doh is C

Trad. adapted N.K.

Fa-la-la

Doh is C

Trad.

SUPPLEMENTARY EXERCISES

Doh is G

1

2

3

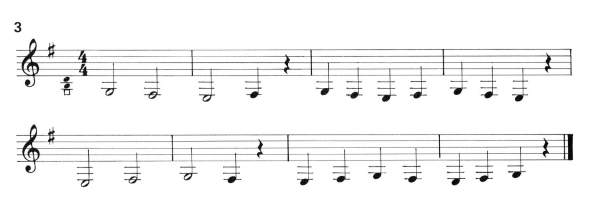

4

5

TUNES

The Submariner's Hornpipe

Doh is G

N.K.

Prowling in the Woods

Doh is G (Key is E minor)

N.K.

Step 11: Throat Notes A and G Sharp

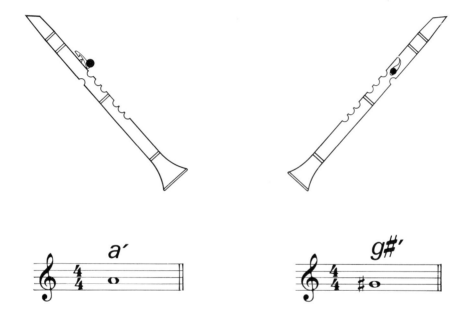

TEACHING NOTES

In the Preliminary Exercises, the student should be shown how to roll (or 'lean') the left hand finger on to the A key, rather than 'jump' on to it. A new key-signature is introduced—D Major with C sharp—although the 'new' note of $c^{\#\prime}$ is not yet needed. If the student does not notice the new signature, a reminder is called for: always look at the key-signature before playing. Some new minor keys are also introduced, which need explanation on the lines of page 47. The difference between melodic and harmonic minor scales is shown (in *sound*) for A minor. There is no need to explain the theory any further than: upwards, raise the seventh in *harmonic* minor but raise the sixth and seventh in *melodic* minor; downwards, play the same in *harmonic* minor, but cancel the ♯ or ♮ on the sixth and seventh in *melodic* minor.

68

DAILY WARM-UP

Doh is C

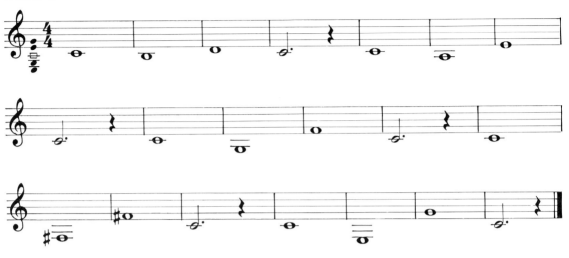

PRELIMINARY EXERCISES

1
Doh is D

2
Doh is D

3
Doh is G

4
Doh is G

5
Doh is G

6
Doh is F (Key is D minor)

7
Doh is C (Key is A minor)

8

9

10   The Scale of A minor (Melodic)

11   The Scale of A minor (Harmonic)

Arpeggio of A minor

TUNES

The Wetley Rocks Waltz

Doh is F   N.K.

Damascus at Dusk

Many Arabic countries use what we call the Harmonic Minor scale as a basis for their tunes.

Doh is C (Key is A minor) N.K.

Fido's Lament

Fido is a more sophisticated dog, using the Melodic Minor scale as a basis for his tune.

Doh is C (Key is A minor) N.K.

Step 12: Slurs, Ties and Phrasing

TEACHING NOTES

Although the Preliminary Exercises are quite easy, the student should play each one many times to get the 'feel' of the phrasing and develop a true cantabile legato. Listening to your demonstration is probably more important at this stage than any up to now.

It may be helpful to demonstrate the difference between a slur and a tie before the value is used in the Preliminary Exercises. You may like to explain the Italian abbreviations for 'loud' and 'soft' in the tunes: *piano (p)* = 'soft'; *forte (f)* = 'loud'; *mezzo (m)* = 'half'.

DAILY WARM-UP

Doh is C

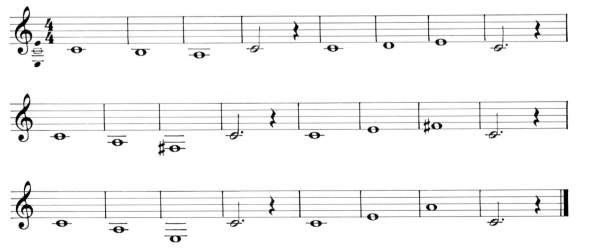

74

PRELIMINARY EXERCISES

1
Doh is G

2
Doh is F

3
Doh is G

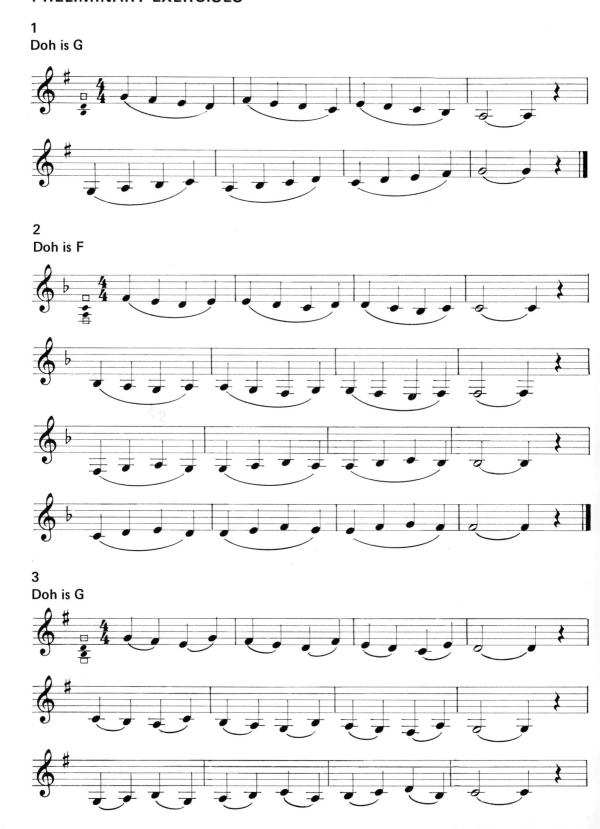

4
Doh is F

5
Doh is G

6

Doh is F

TUNES

The Grosvenor Gavotte

Doh is C

N.K.

The Hybrid Gavotte

In this tune, explain the use of 'hairpins', which open or close *gradually*.

Doh is G

N.K.

A Courtly Dance

Doh is C

N.K.

Rule, Britannia

Doh is C

Adapted from the original of T. Arne, 1710 - 1778

SUPPLEMENTARY EXERCISES

1
Doh is F

2
Doh is G

3
Doh is F

TUNES

Drink to me only

Doh is G   18th-century Glee

at *FINE* only

Valse Claire

Doh is C   N.K.

Step 13:   The Value ♩·

TEACHING NOTES

The new rhythm is introduced by way of a tie from ♩ to ♪ in the First Preliminary Exercise. Before going on to the second, recall the definition of 𝅗𝅥· on page 16, asking the student to define the ♩· in the same way. *Thinking* a tie is a good way to start playing the ♩· in time but make sure the student does not put any accent on the second note of the imaginary tie.

The daily warm-up provides an opportunity to discuss correct breathing with the student who, with persistence, should discover how to make a *crescendo* sound (='increasing', *ie* ⏤⏤⏤) without blowing harder. Take care that there is no lowering of pitch in the crescendos.

DAILY WARM-UP

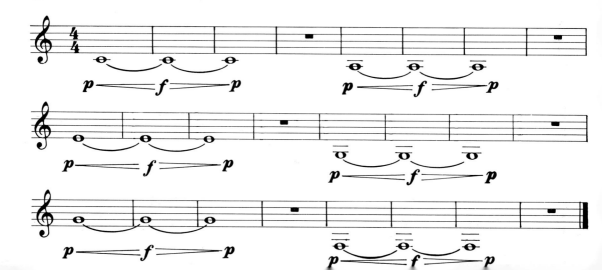

PRELIMINARY EXERCISES

Doh is C

82

TUNES

All through the Night

Doh is C

Trad.

A Drinking Song

Doh is F

N.K.

Allegro Maestoso

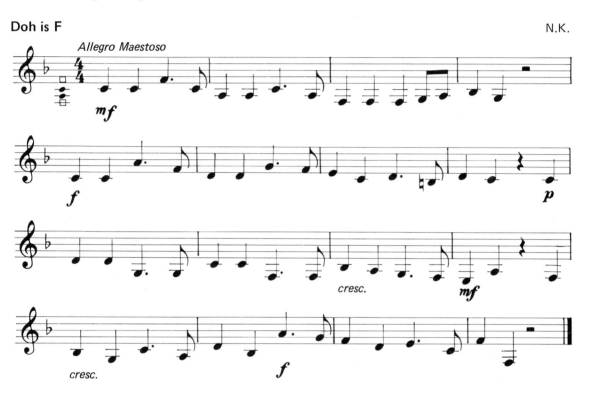

SUPPLEMENTARY EXERCISE

Doh is C

TUNES

Men of Harlech

Doh is C

Trad.

Lilliburlero

Doh is G

17th-century ballad

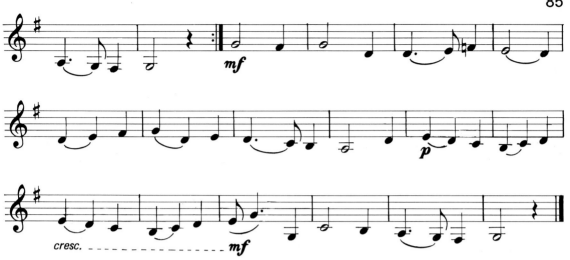

Scarborough Fair

Doh is B flat (Key is G minor)

Trad.

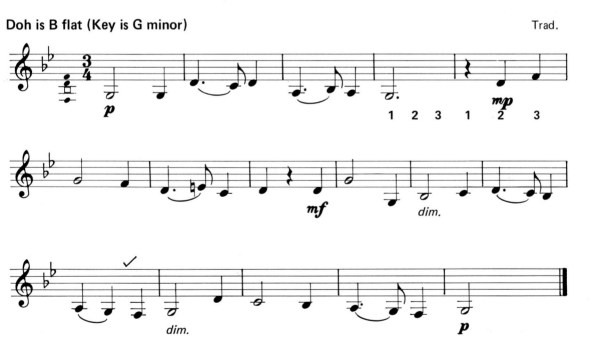

When you can play this tune by heart follow it with *The Coventry Carol* (page 47) and listen to the different 'minor' effects.

Cockles and Mussels

Doh is C

Trad.

Step 14: C Sharp and D Flat

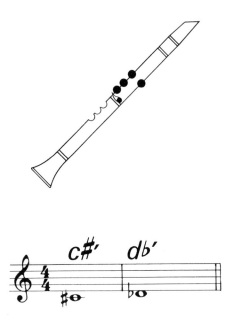

TEACHING NOTES

The Preliminary Exercises are much easier than they look, though students may need some convincing and it will be helpful to demonstrate one or two first.

The massive key-signature of *Dirgery-Doo* may seem similarly frightening, but by checking the notes used against the signature it will soon be appreciated that *b, d'* and *a* are the only three notes to be played flat unless otherwise indicated by ♮. If the solfa symbols at the beginning are sung *and played* first, the key sound will rest in the ear. The same applies to the tunes in A major: play the solfa arpeggio first to fix the key in the ear.

Be ready for the conducting lessons in *Shenandoah* and *The Minstrel Boy.*

DAILY WARM-UP

Doh is C

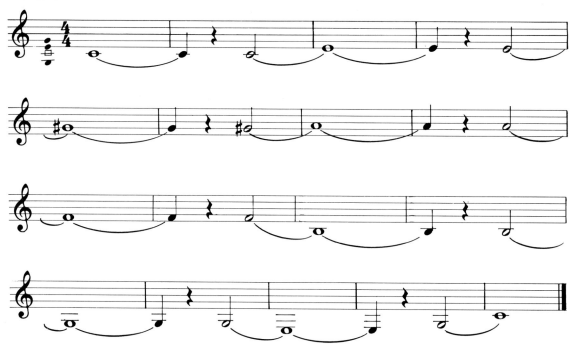

PRELIMINARY EXERCISES

1

2

7

TUNE

Dirgery-Doo

Doh is D flat (Key is B flat minor)   N.K.

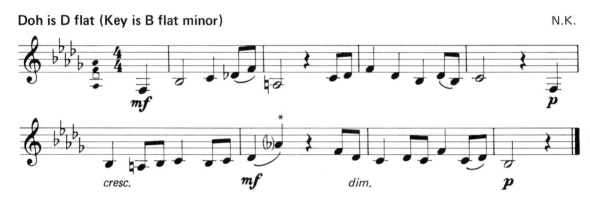

* Fingering for $a^{b\prime}$ is the same as $g^{\#\prime}$ (see Step 11).

SUPPLEMENTARY EXERCISES

1   The Scale of A major

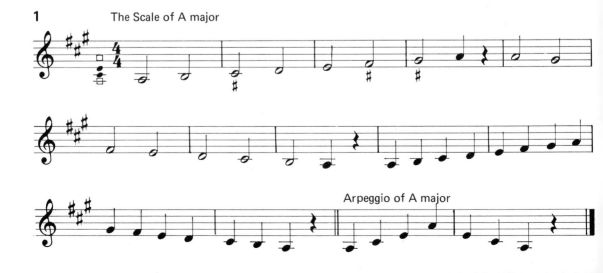

2   The Scale of A major stepwise

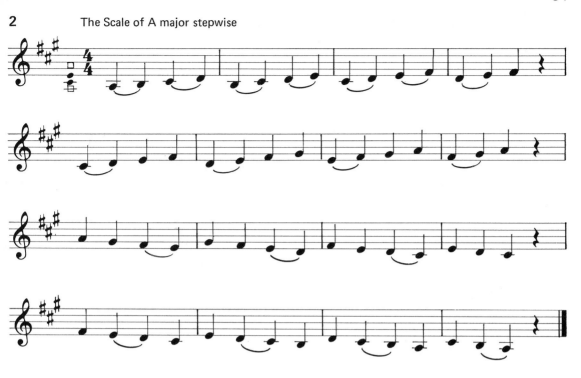

TUNES

Nicola's Waltz

Doh is A   N.K.

Auld Lang Syne

Doh is A

Trad.

Shenandoah

Note that the time changes, *ie* the number of beats in a bar is not the same throughout. It may help to explain how a conductor beats 4-in-a-bar and 3-in-a-bar, so that students can understand this when they first play in an orchestra or band.

Doh is A

Trad. Sea Shanty

The Minstrel Boy

Look carefully ($\large\frownie$ $\frownie$) at bars 7 and 8. What kind of F starts each bar?

The sign $\frownie$ in bar 8 is a pause: hang on to the note a little longer than $\quarternote$; then take a quick breath and play on in strict time. When students play in any ensemble, someone will have to act as 'conductor' so that everyone holds the pause for the same length *and* moves off together. This can be shown by using the instrument itself, taking everyone off the pause by a short 'wave' of the bell and going on with a small 'up-beat' of the bell. Be prepared to demonstrate.

Doh is A

Trad.

Step 15: E Flat and D Sharp

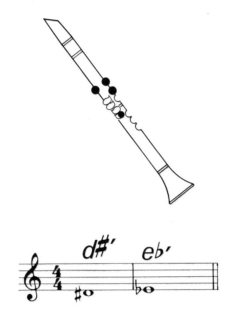

TEACHING NOTES

This step treats the new fingering first as $e^{b\prime}$ (using the keys of B♭ major and G minor), then as $d^{\#\prime}$ (using the keys of B major and E minor). The Preliminary Exercises are intended for the side key $e^{b\prime}/d^{\#\prime}$ fingering: the left hand fourth-finger $e^{b\prime}/d^{\#\prime}$ is left for the chromatic scale in Step 19. The Boehm fingering may be used in the last four bars of the third Preliminary Exercise and the first Supplementary Exercise but the intonation may prove unsatisfactory.

DAILY WARM-UP

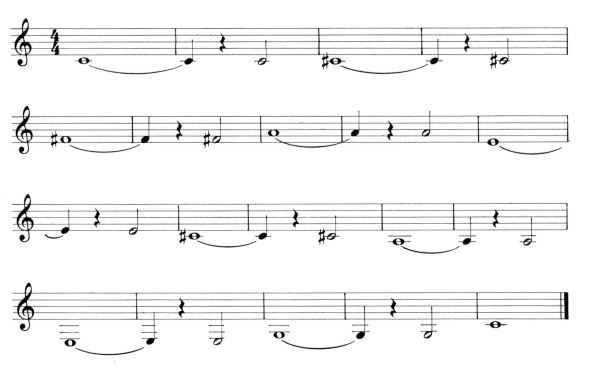

PRELIMINARY EXERCISES

1

2

3

4

Doh is D flat (Key is B flat minor)

5

Doh is B flat (Key is G minor)

The Scale of G minor (Melodic)

Arpeggio of G minor

6 The Scale of G minor (Harmonic)

Arpeggio of G minor

7 The Scale of G minor (Melodic) stepwise

In broken thirds

TUNES

Toucan Tango

Two new things to remember: a dot under a note makes it *staccato* (= 'detached') from its neighbour: a short horizontal makes the note *tenuto* (= 'held on') to its neighbour.

Doh is B flat (Key is G minor)   N.K.

Bach's Byte

Doh is B flat (Key is G minor)   N.K.

SUPPLEMENTARY EXERCISES

1
Doh is B

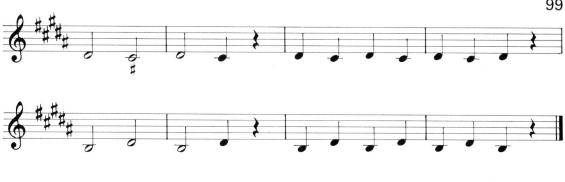

2
Doh is B

3
Doh is G (Key is E minor)

The Scale of E minor (Melodic)

Arpeggio of E minor

4   The Scale of E minor (Melodic) stepwise

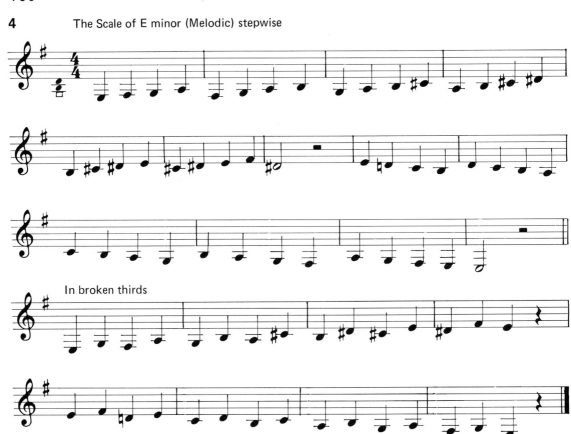

In broken thirds

5   The Scale of E minor (Harmonic)

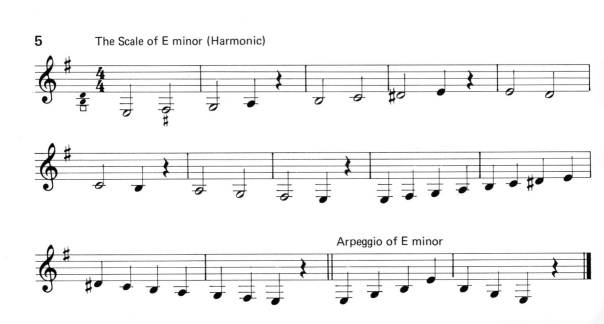

Arpeggio of E minor

TUNE

Valse Volage

Doh is G (Key is E minor)

N.K.

Step 16: Throat B Flat

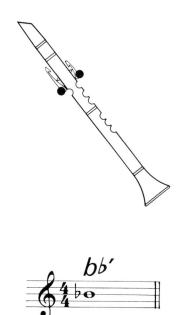

bb'

TEACHING NOTES

The wider the interval, the more difficult it is to keep the tone matching and steady. In this warm-up, the intervals are widened gradually to highlight the difficulty. The main thing to emphasise is that there should be *no* movement of the embouchure.

The Preliminary Exercises are to help left hand thumb facility. Make sure from the beginning that the student presses the speaker key in such a way so that the thumb may return to the thumb hole by rolling, not sliding. This is vital to the third Exercise.

The Supplementary Exercise introduces the third flat in the key of E♭ and it should be explained that $a^{b\prime}$ has the same fingering as $g^{\#\prime}$ (as in Steps 11 and 14).

DAILY WARM-UP

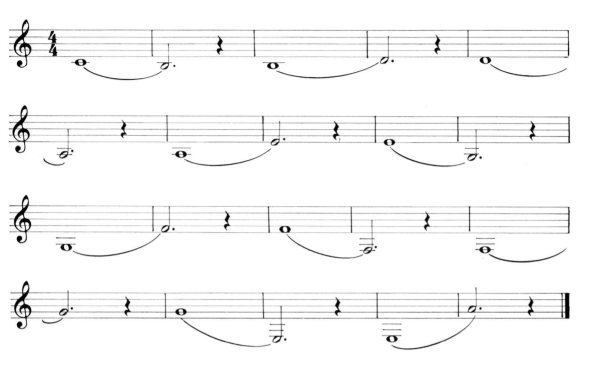

PRELIMINARY EXERCISES

1
Doh is B flat (Key is G minor)

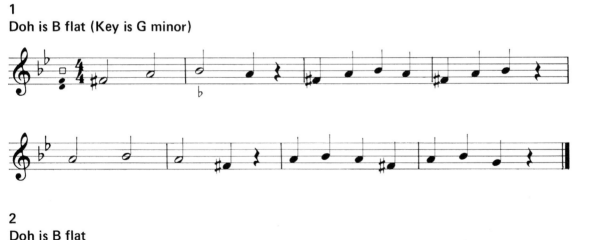

2
Doh is B flat

3
Doh is B flat

4
Doh is E flat

5 The Scale of B flat major

Arpeggio of B flat major

6 The Scale of B flat major, stepwise

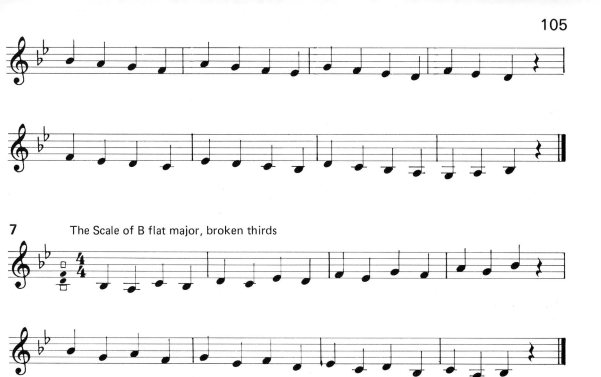

7   The Scale of B flat major, broken thirds

TUNES

Believe me, if all those endearing young charms

Doh is B flat   18th-century ballad

Fair Phyllis

Doh is B flat

N.K.

Tina's Tune

Doh is B flat

N.K.

SUPPLEMENTARY EXERCISE

Doh is E flat

TUNES

Country Dance

Doh is E flat

N.K.

A Short Minuet

Doh is B flat (Key is G minor)

J.S. Bach, 1685 - 1750

A Long Minuet

Doh is B flat (Key is G minor)

J.S. Bach, 1685 - 1750

Step 17: Low G Sharp

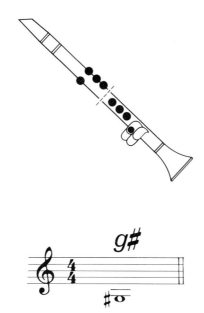

g♯

TEACHING NOTES

Although low *g♯* and *a♭* share common fingering, they are here divided between two steps so that the student may become familiar with the remaining 'sharp' and 'flat' keys separately. Note that in E major Supplementary Exercises the left-hand *f♯* is used with right-hand bottom *E*. Warning about changing fingers (right to left hand) will be advisable in *The Camels are coming* for the quick-change bottom *f* in bar 7.

DAILY WARM-UP

PRELIMINARY EXERCISES

1

2

3

4

TUNE

David of the White Rock

Doh is C (Key is A minor)

Trad. Welsh

112

SUPPLEMENTARY EXERCISE

TUNE

Greensleeves

Doh is C (Key is A minor)

SUPPLEMENTARY EXERCISES

1

2 The Scale of E major

Arpeggio of E major

3 The Scale of E major, stepwise

114

4 The Scale of E major, broken thirds

TUNE

Home, Sweet Home

Doh is E

Trad. adapted N.K.

SUPPLEMENT EXERCISE

Doh is C (Key is A minor)

TUNES

The Camels are coming

Doh is C (Key is A minor)   N.K.

Syrian Sunset

Doh is C (Key is A minor)   N.K.

Step 18: Low A Flat

TEACHING NOTES

The warm-up is designed to guard against the nasal sound which can result on low $a^\flat/g^\sharp$ from a slack embouchure. Evenness of tone remains paramount. In the Supplementary Exercises, remind students of the alternative fingerings for f and $g^\flat$ when they come before $a^\flat$.

In *A Flat Rock* and *Get Well Soon Blues*, check that—in finding the right pop or jazz idiom—no coarse tone or bad intonation creeps in.

DAILY WARM-UP

PRELIMINARY EXERCISES

Doh is A flat

1

2

3   The Scale of A flat major

Arpeggio of A flat major

4   The Scale of A flat major, stepwise

5   The Scale of A flat major, broken thirds

TUNES

To a Wild Rose

D. C. (Da Capo) means 'from the start' (see page 25). Play to the sign ⊕ and then play the *Coda* (='tailpiece').

Doh is A flat

E. MacDowell, 1861 - 1908

A Flat Rock

Doh is A flat

N.K.

SUPPLEMENTARY EXERCISES

1

2

3

R

L R

4 The Scale of F minor (Melodic)

Arpeggio of F minor

L

5 The Scale of F minor (Harmonic)

Arpeggio of F minor

6 The Scale of F minor (Melodic), stepwise

7 The Scale of F minor (Melodic), broken thirds

TUNE

Get Well Soon Blues

Doh is A flat (Key is F minor)

N.K.

Simple Variation

*Cadenza (optional)

* A cadenza was often improvised in classical music from the 18th century onwards, towards the end of a movement, and the custom migrated to the end of a series of jazz improvisations. This cadenza is a 'written-out improvisation' to be played *extempore* (='out of time'), *ie* as freely as the students enjoy it.

Step 19: The Chromatic Scale

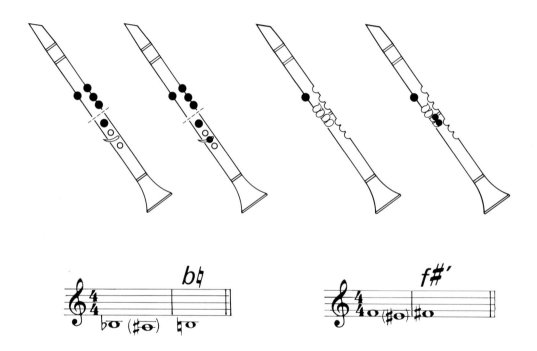

TEACHING NOTES

This step reaches the special chromatic fingering for $b^\flat$–$b^\natural$ and $f^\natural{}'$–$f^\sharp{}'$. At this stage, too, students may be shown the alternative (or you might consider it the principal) fingering for $e^{\flat}{}'/d^{\sharp}{}'$ using the left hand fourth finger. In the warm-up, see that the student absorbs that $g^\flat$ is the same as $f^\sharp$ and $c^{\flat}{}'$ the same as $b^\natural$: and in the first Preliminary Exercise that $c^{\natural}{}'$ in bar 3 might have been written $b^\sharp$. One more note to make is that the chromatic fingering $a^\sharp$–b cannot be used in bar 15 of *Gaudy Waltz*.

DAILY WARM-UP

PRELIMINARY EXERCISES

1

2

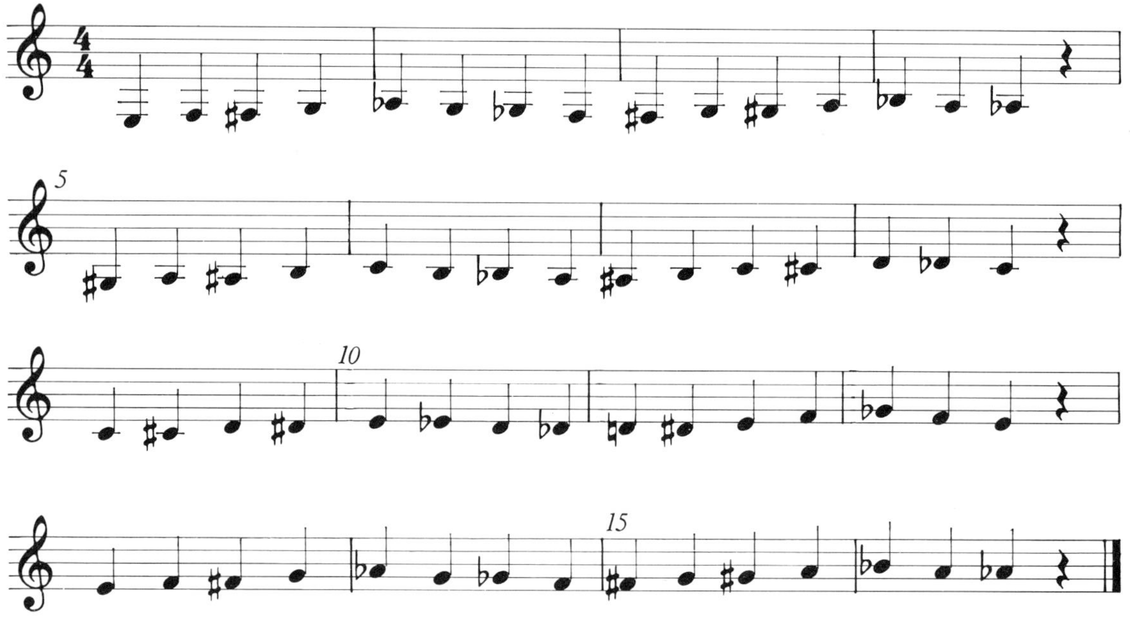

3

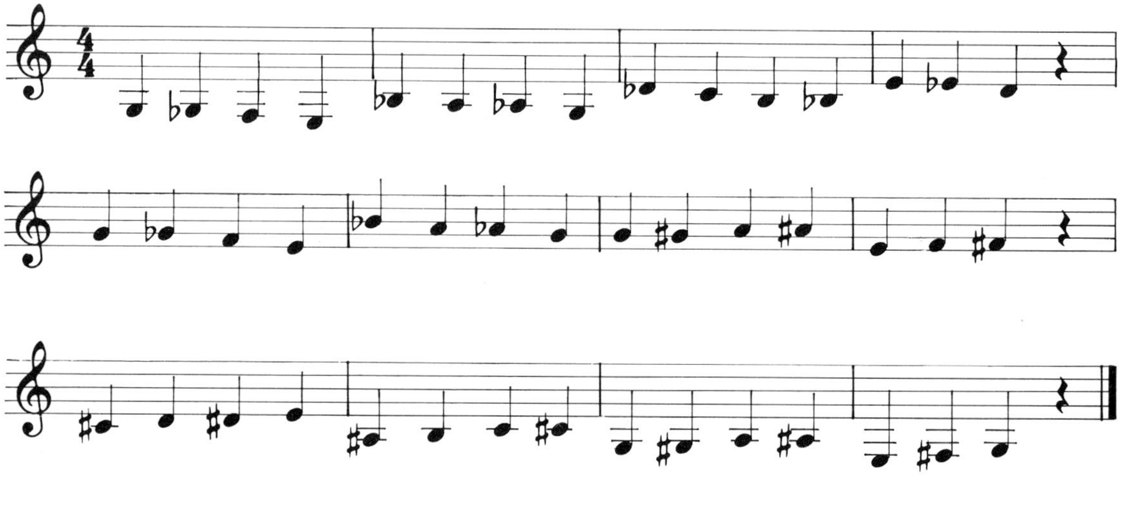

4

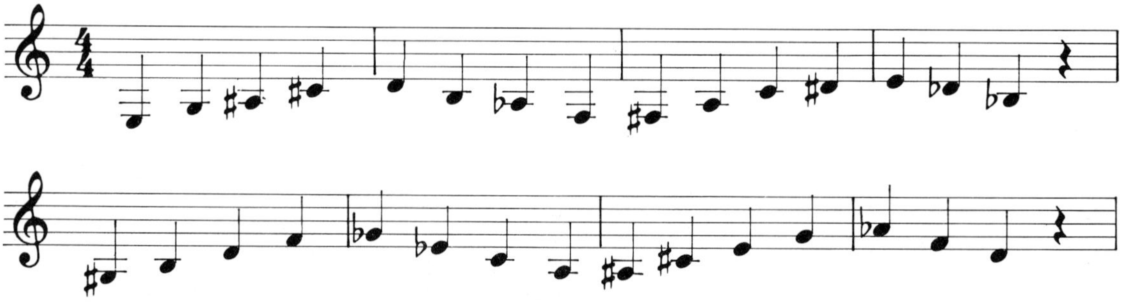

TUNES

Gaudy Waltz

Doh is G N.K.

Rock Solid

Doh is G N.K.

Step 20: The Clarion Register I

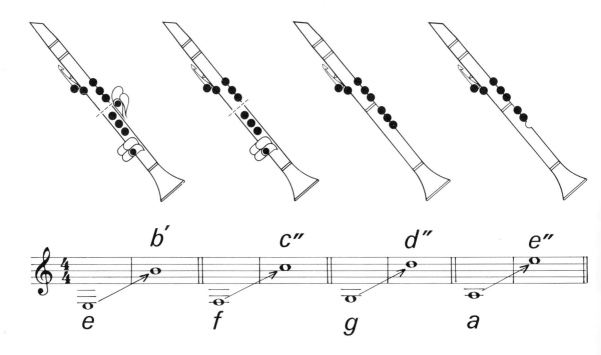

TEACHING NOTES

Explain that this high but not extreme clarinet register owes its name to an 18th-century description of notes in this register sounding 'from afar, like a trumpet'. Some may call it the *clarino* register. To complete the student's knowledge of clarinet terms, explain also about the word *chalumeau* (= 'reed', used to describe the popular reed instrument which was developed into the clarinet, c. 1700) for the lowest register. Students should by now have had sufficient practice to develop a reliable embouchure and no extra effort should be needed to 'overblow' for the clarion register. The first three Preliminary Exercises develop ease in using the speaker key, an essential requisite for 'crossing the break' (*a'* to *b'*) smoothly; the fourth and fifth exercises use the easy way to cross the break, downwards; and the last two use the more difficult crossing.

Slurs are used to encourage students to change fingerings quickly and easily.

DAILY WARM-UP

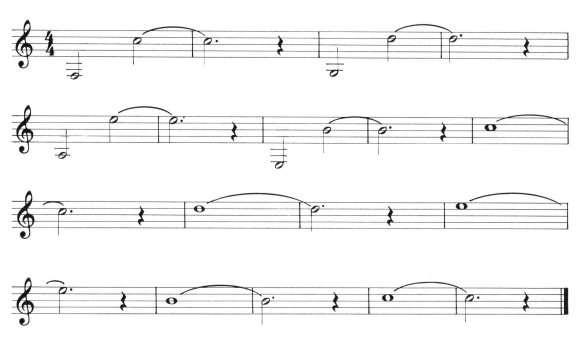

PRELIMINARY EXERCISES

1

2

Doh is C

3

4

5
Doh is C

6
Doh is C (Key is A minor)

7

Doh is G

8   The Scale of C major

Arpeggio of C major

The Scale of C major, stepwise 1

The Scale of C major, stepwise 2

The Scale of C major, broken thirds

TUNES

Adeste Fideles

Doh is G

18th-century carol hymn

David Franklin's Fancie

Doh is C

N.K.

Bobby Shaftoe

Doh is G

Trad. Sea Shanty

Country Gardens

Doh is C

Trad. adapted N.K.

Step 21: Clarion Register II

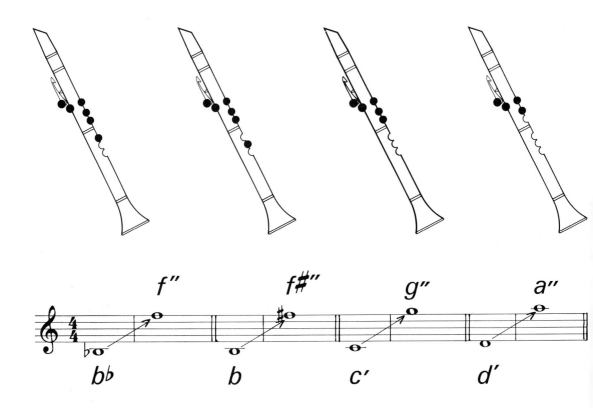

TEACHING NOTES

In this step, students practise crossing the break from $b^{b\prime}$ to c''. Squeaking may be expected to begin with, usually caused by the clumsy left hand thumb. Even though the student will be preoccupied with this new obstacle, insist that equality of tone between the registers is the constant aim: the throat register $b^{b\prime}$ need not be less prominent but should match the tone of a' and c''.

DAILY WARM-UP

PRELIMINARY EXERCISES

1

Doh is C

138

2
Doh is F

3
Doh is F

4 The Scale of F major

Arpeggio of F major   The Scale of F major, stepwise

The Scale of F major, broken thirds

TUNES

Austrian Hymn

Doh is F

Franz Joseph Haydn, 1732 - 1809

On Wings of Song

Doh is F

Felix Mendelssohn, 1809 - 1847

Step 22: The Full Range

TEACHING NOTES

The 'new' notes, completing the clarion register to high *c''*, take the student's range to about Grade 3 level. After the Daily Warm-ups and a Preliminary Exercise on the chromatic scale, exercises are given on all the scales set for Grade 3. As the various examining bodies differ in the form of these scale requirements, however, it is wise to check with the particular syllabus as soon as the extended scale exercises here are secure in the student's memory.

DAILY WARM-UP 1

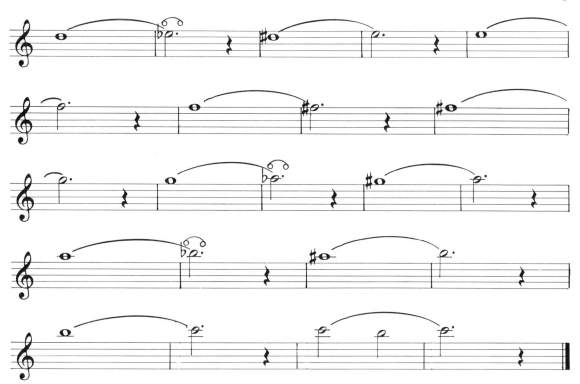

DAILY WARM-UP 2

The Scale of C major, stepwise

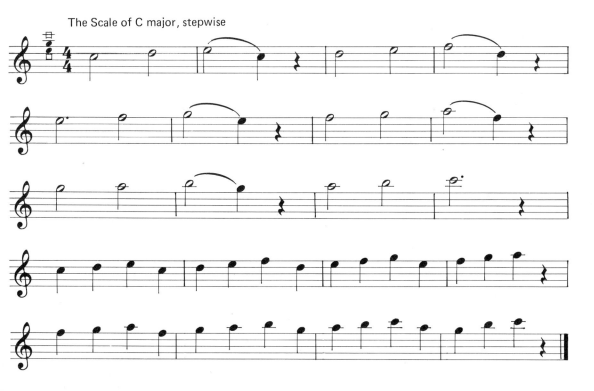

PRELIMINARY EXERCISES

Doh is C

1

2 The extended Scale of C major

Extended arpeggio of C major

3 The extended Scale of F major

Extended arpeggio of F major

4   The extended Scale of G major

Extended arpeggio of G major

5   The extended Scale of A minor (Melodic)

The extended Scale of A minor (Harmonic)

Extended arpeggio of A minor

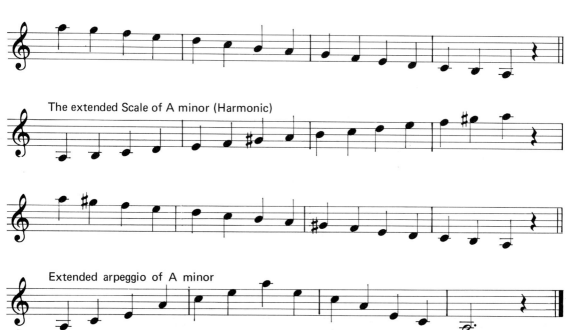

6 The extended Scale of G minor (Melodic)

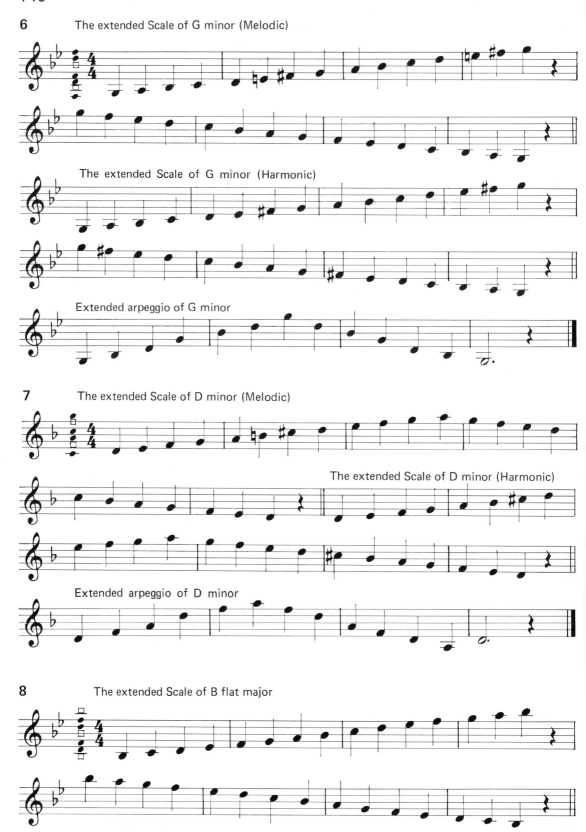

The extended Scale of G minor (Harmonic)

Extended arpeggio of G minor

7 The extended Scale of D minor (Melodic)

The extended Scale of D minor (Harmonic)

Extended arpeggio of D minor

8 The extended Scale of B flat major

TUNES

The Liquorice Stick Rag

Doh is G

N.K.

Valse Finale

Doh is C

N.K.

With the firm practice ground provided by these steps, students should now be ready to take off individually to whatever heights they may aspire. The inner hearing of solfa will help intonation for ever and, as they should now be able to write from memory (or by ear with the clarinet as a reminder) 98 tunes, reading at sight and playing by ear should present few problems if future progress is as methodical!